IRA CRUMB
Feels the Feelings

All of them!

For my brother Roy. You always know how to make me laugh—N.H.

IRA CRUMB
Feels the Feelings

Written by Naseem Hrab & Illustrated by Josh Holinaty

Population: ME!

OWLKIDS BOOKS

This is Ira Crumb.
And this is Malcolm Cake.

They both have delicious last names.
And they're best friends.

Ira and Malcolm always make each other laugh.

Ira and Malcolm always eat lunch together.

And Ira and Malcolm always play together.

Maybe Ira and Malcolm don't always play together.

BRIIP!

Ahem...

And so they did.